Free to Be Me

Songs **Sunflowers** Illustrations **Maud Legrand**

1 My Heart

Sometimes my heart feels happy
I smile here, I smile there, everywhere

Sometimes my heart feels sad
Stormy skies, rainy cheeks, cloudy eyes

Sometimes my heart feels scared
I close my eyes and fly up high to the sky

My heart can feel everything, everything

Sometimes my heart feels mad
I get hot and stomp my feet, hear my heart beat

Sometimes my heart feels shy
I like to hide behind my hands, find me if you can

Sometimes my heart feels proud
I stand up tall and beat my chest, I feel like the best

My heart can feel everything, everything

Good morning to the boys
Good morning to the girls
Good morning to the people all around the world
Today is a beautiful day

Stand up tall and turn around
Wave your hands and please sit down
Close your eyes and breathe in now
Very slowly breathe out

Good morning to the birds
Good morning to the bees
Good morning to the fish in the big blue sea
Today is a beautiful day

③ Family

F-A-M-I-L-Y
This is mommy, she is small
This is daddy, he is tall
This is brother, he is taller
This is sister, she is smaller
This is baby, he is tiny
And he's sleeping
Tonight

❹ Be Brave Not Afraid

I can be brave
I can be courageous
I can be strong
I can be adventurous
I can be bold
I can be fearless
I can be calm
I can be audacious
I'll be brave and not afraid

Can you be brave?
Can you be courageous?
Can you be strong?
Can you be adventurous?
Can you be bold?
Can you be fearless?
Can you be calm?
Can you be audacious?
Just be brave and not afraid

You can be brave
You can be courageous
You can be strong
You can be adventurous
You can be bold
You can be fearless
You can be audacious
Just be brave and not afraid

❺ What Do You Want to Be?

What do I want to be?
I can be anything I want to be
Don't tell me what I can't be
I can be anything I want to be

A doctor, a football player
Or a barber who cuts hair
A firefighter or a writer
Maybe just a basketball player

What do I want to be?
I can be anything I want to be
Don't tell me what I can't be
I can be anything I want to be

A businessman, an engineer
Maybe I'll be a volunteer
A musician or a chef
Whatever it is, I'll do my best

What do you want to be?
You can be anything you want to be
Don't tell me what you can't be
You can be anything you want to be

A translator or a waiter
Or a zoo keeper with alligators
I could fly a plane with wings
Or an architect who builds things

What do you want to be?
You can be anything you want to be
Don't tell me what you can't be
You can be anything you want to be

❻ Days of the Week

Monday
Tuesday
Wednesday
Thursday
I love Friday
Saturday and Sunday

Seven days in a week
Ten toes on my feet
Ten fingers on my hands
Two eyes to see
One tongue to sing

7 Orchestra

Hey boy, hey boy, what do you hear?
I hear a guitar singing to me

Hey girl, hey girl, what do you hear?
I hear a trumpet singing to me

Hey boy, hey boy, what do you hear?
I hear a bongo singing to me

Hey girl, hey girl, what do you hear?
I hear a bass drum singing to me

I hear an orchestra
I hear an orchestra

Hey boy, hey boy, what do you hear?
I hear a violin singing to me

Hey girl, hey girl, what do you hear?
I hear a cello singing to me

Hey boy, hey boy, what do you hear?
I hear a piano singing to me

Hey girl, hey girl, what do you hear?
I hear a harmonica singing to me

I hear an orchestra
I hear an orchestra

8 Small or Tall

I'm very, very small
I'm very, very tall
Sometimes small
Sometimes tall
What am I now?
What am I now?

I'm moving slowly
I'm moving quickly
Sometimes slowly
Sometimes quickly
How am I moving now?
How am I moving now?

My hand is on my arm
Now under my arm
Sometimes on
Sometimes under
Where is it now?
Where is it now?

9 The Color Song

I see blue
I see red
I see colors in my head

I see black
I see white
I see the stars in the night

I see yellow
I see green
I want to be king or queen

I see purple
I see pink
Do you want to eat or drink?

I see orange
I see brown
I can stand up and sit down

I see a rainbow in the sky
Now it's time to say goodbye

⑩ Together

I am happy to be with Y-O-U
You, you
Can you tell me where you want to G-O
Go, go
You can wish upon a star with M-E
Me, me
Or just sit under a T-R-E-E
Tree, tree

I run, I run around the sun
You hide behind the Flint hillsides
She got me, now I'll get her
To be to be together

I swim, I swim out to sea
She shot a rainbow right at me
Count to ten and we'll begin
To be together once again

Three little words come together
You plus me equals together
Three little words come together
You plus me equals together
Always together
Always together

11 Goodbye

Goodbye
Goodbye
Goodbye
See you next time

ABCDEFG
HIJKLMNOP
QRS
TUV
WX
YZ
Now I said my ABCs
Next time
Won't you sing with me?

⑫ Go to Sleep Tonight

Go to sleep tonight
You can close your eyes
I'll always be right by your side
Go to sleep tonight

I sing your favorite song
While you sing along
I'll always be right by your side
Go to sleep tonight

You're a miracle
Those big blue eyes
So pure and beautiful
Forever mine

Go to sleep tonight
The stars are shining bright
I'll always be right by your side
Go to sleep tonight

Tonight
Tonight
Tonight

Activity guide

How to use the guide

Discover themes, learn how to express emotions, and play educational games with the activity guide. Lessons for each song are presented in the following format.

Overview

Read a brief description to see what type of song it is and how it might interest young learners.

Discover the song

Before you play the song, share these prompts and listening instructions. These cues put the song in a particular context so learners can explore language, music, and other related learning concepts.

Activity

After listening to the song, encourage active engagement with a learning activity. Explained in simple terms, these activities provide learners with opportunities to express themselves and deepen their understanding. Of course, each exercise should be adapted to your specific teaching and learning context.

One step further

When you've particularly enjoyed the song and activity, go one step further with an extra challenge. These exercises and activities are designed to reinforce vocabulary, language skills, and promote self-expression.

 My Heart

Overview

This twangy tune gives little ones the chance to explore their full range of emotions. An action or description accompanies each sentiment so they can discover ways to express or process each feeling.

Discover the song

Invite young listeners to pay attention to the song's lyrics and try to remember all the emotions they hear. Make a list of the emotions they remember after a first listen, then complete the list after a second listen.

Activity

Stand up and perform the actions described in the second line of each verse. Before playing the song, determine together how you will act out each line. For example, for the line "I smile here, I smile there, everywhere," you could smile to the right, left, and then in a half-circle. For a more abstract line like "Stormy skies, rainy cheeks, cloudy eyes," come up with gestures like twinkle fingers.

One step further

Now that you've learned how to express when you feel happy, sad, scared, mad, shy, and proud, share some other emotions your hearts feel. Once you come up with a few suggestions, imagine how you would express these feelings.

❷ A Beautiful Day

Overview

Start every day off on the right note with this celebratory song filled with greetings and optimism.

Discover the song

The second verse includes morning stretching instructions. Prepare listeners to move along with the lyrics by standing up tall, waving their hands, sitting down, breathing in, and breathing out.

Activity

The singers offer morning greetings to many people and creatures throughout the song, including boys, girls, birds, and bees. Discuss the people and animals you could offer greetings to on the way to school or on a trip to the grocery store and create your own verse!

Good morning to the _____
Good morning to the _____
Good morning to the people all around the world
Today is a beautiful day

One step further

Spread greetings throughout the day. Discuss how you would change the song lyrics for the middle and end of the day. Write a new verse for the afternoon and evening.

Good afternoon to the _____
Good afternoon to the _____
Good afternoon to the people all around the world
Today is a beautiful day

Good night to the _____
Good night to the _____
Good night to the people all around the world
Today was a beautiful day

③ Family

Overview

Learn how to spell and compare size and height in this upbeat duet that's all about family relationships.

Discover the song

In addition to family members, this song includes descriptive adjectives. As you listen to the song together, identify all the descriptive words such as "tall" and "taller."

Activity

Draw a picture of your family. You can even add pets or extended family members! Try your best to depict the size and height differences. For example, mommy or daddy is probably taller than you! Once the drawing is finished, label each family member.

One step further

An adjective is used to modify or describe a noun. In the following sentence, "soft" is an adjective used to describe a cat: *The cat is soft*. A comparative adjective is used to compare a person or thing to another person or thing. In the following sentence, "softer" is used to compare a cat to a dog: *My cat is softer than my dog*.

Use descriptive and comparative adjectives from the song to describe your family picture. For example: Which family member is **tall**? Which family member is **taller** than you? Which family member is **smaller** than your mother or father?

④ Be Brave Not Afraid

Overview

This empowering ditty offers children a vocabulary for bravery. It's normal to be afraid sometimes, but we can also be calm, strong, and brave in all sorts of ways.

Discover the song

In the illustration that accompanies the song, a little girl is getting ready to dive into a pool. She's courageous! Make a list of some other activities that require courage.

Activity

Create your own emoticons! Draw six circles of the same size on a piece of paper. Underneath each circle, write an emotion. Choose feelings from the song, or come up with other feelings such as happy, sad, or surprised. Then draw the faces!

One step further

As Mr. Rogers once said, when we talk about our feelings, they become less overwhelming, upsetting, and scary. Use the prompts below to share a personal story. Share them on your own, with a partner, or in a group.

Tell us about a time when you were **brave**.

Have you ever remained **calm**, even though you were afraid?

What does being **strong** mean to you?

⑤ What Do You Want to Be?

Overview

Inspire young dreamers to imagine what they will be when they grow up with this pop-rock anthem, which includes the refrain: "I can be anything I want to be."

Discover the song

Explain to listeners that this song is about different occupations. Ask them to listen to the lyrics and the different types of jobs mentioned.

Activity

Create a list of all the occupations in the song. Can you think of others? Add as many as you can! Then, decide which one is your favorite! Remember, you can be anything you want to be, no matter your gender, background, or location.

One step further

Draw your dream job! Imagine what type of uniform or work clothes you'd have to wear. What kind of tools or equipment would you need to do this job? What would your workplace look like?

6 Days of the Week

Overview

Clap along to this jaunty tune, which gets learners to repeat the days of the week and branches off into numbers and the names of body parts.

Discover the song

With a calendar in front of you, point out each day of the week when it's mentioned in the song. Notice how, in North America, calendars begin with Sunday as the first day of the week and end with Saturday.

Activity

Question time! Listen carefully to the song. Can you find the answers to all of the questions below?

- How many days are there in a week?
- How many toes do most people have on their feet?
- How many fingers do most people have on their hands?
- How many eyes do you have?
- How many tongues do you have?

Bonus Question:

- There are the same amount of days in a weekend as most people have eyes. How many days are there in a weekend?

One step further

Come up with your own answers!

- Why do you think the singer says, "I love Friday"?
- On what day of the week are you the most awake? The most tired?
- What is your favorite day of the week? Why?
- If you were asked to create a new day of the week, what would you name it?

Answers: seven; ten; ten; two; one; two: Saturday and Sunday.

 Orchestra

Overview

Sing along with this acoustic call-and-response song as it lists different musical instruments.

Discover the song

An orchestra is a large group of musicians that plays together. Listen carefully for the different instruments mentioned in the lyrics and make a list.

Activity

Look at the instruments instruments pictured below. Can you identify all five of them? What other instruments are mentioned in the song lyrics? Can you think of any others? If you could join an orchestra, which instrument would you like to play?

One step further

The instruments of an orchestra are grouped into different musical families, such as string and percussion. Can you match the instruments in the illustration to each one?

String
String family instruments include strings and are played with fingers or bows.

Percussion
Percussion family instruments are played by shaking or striking them with hands or sticks.

Brass
Brass instruments are often made of yellow metal and are played by blowing air.

Keyboard
The keyboard family includes instruments that make notes when keys are played.

Woodwind
Woodwind family instruments are often made of wood and are played by blowing air.

Answers: 1. Trumpet (brass), 2. Keyboard (keyboard), 3. Guitar (string), 4. Harmonica (woodwind), 5. Bongo (percussion)

 Small or Tall

Overview

With deliberately paced lines, this song helps reinforce adjectives that relate to height and size, such as **small** or **tall**. It also introduces simple adverbs (**slowly** and **quickly**) and prepositions (**on** and **under**).

Discover the song

Practice the vocabulary through various actions. Prompt young learners to do the following:

- Stand up **tall**.
- Make yourself **small**.
- Move **slowly** across the room.
- Move **quickly** in place.
- Place your hand **on** your arm.
- Place your hand **under** your arm.

Activity

Once you have mastered the actions, play the song again. Perform the actions when the singer comes to each of the bolded words.

One step further

A preposition is a word that shows direction and location. Sometimes these words are also used to introduce an object. Master words like **on**, **over**, and **under** with a game of Preposition Simon Says.

Simon says... Put your hands **over** your eyes
Simon says... Sit down **on** the floor
Simon says... Stick one leg **in front** of you
Simon says... Put your hands **under** your chin
Simon says... Put your hands **on** your head
Simon says... Put one hand **behind** your back
Simon says... Put your index finger **on** your nose

9 The Color Song

Overview

Accentuated by harmonica, this jangly ode to color speeds up near the end, offering vibrant lyrics in two different tempos.

Discover the song

Listen to all the colors mentioned in the song: blue, red, black, white, yellow, green, purple, pink, orange, brown. Then look around the room. Can you find all the colors? What colors are the hardest to find?

Activity

Turn to the illustration that accompanies the song. Now that you're a color expert, see if you can answer these questions:

What color is the boy's crown?
What color is the boy's hair?
What color are the boy's cheeks?
What color is the boy's shirt?
What color are the boy's pants?
What color is the cauldron?
What color is the bowl?

One step further

Time for a color scavenger hunt! Flip through the pages of the book to see if you can find the following:

A red flag
A pink bird
A brown guitar
A grey cat
A green alligator
A white sailboat
A blue keyboard
A yellow star
An orange fence
A black box
A purple hill

⑩ Together

Overview

This laid-back surf rock song offers an array of different lessons, including an opportunity to practice spelling and a chance to appreciate the concept of togetherness.

Discover the song

When letters of the alphabet come together in the correct order, they form words. Tell young learners to listen for the words that the singer spells out, including **you**, **go**, **me**, and **tree**.

Activity

On notecards, write out the letters Y, O, U, G, M, T, R, and two E's (one letter per card). Then, scatter the notecards in front of you. Now ask them to spell out the following words:

- "you" (Y-O-U)
- "go" (G-O)
- "me" (M-E)
- "tree" (T-R-E-E)

To modify this activity for a group or classroom, write each letter on a board and ask learners to spell out words together aloud or on a piece of paper.

One step further

On your own or with a partner, see how many more words you can spell out with the same letters. Add a few more letter cards to make it easier. We recommend S, A, L, I, and N. Use each letter as many times as you want in a single word. For example: rug, tug, gum, root, met, meet.

Make it a game! Form teams and see which one can come up with the most words!

⑪ Goodbye

Overview

This alphabet farewell tune bids listeners adieu with the refrain: "Goodbye! See you next time."

Discover the song

In this song, one voice sings the goodbye refrain, while another sings the ABCs. Pick one part to sing along to the first time you listen. The next time, sing the other part!

Activity

G is for Goodbye. Create your own alphabet vocabulary by finding words for each letter of the alphabet. Need some help? Look through this book or pick up one near you to find words.

A is for ...
B is for ...
C is for ...

Hint: Xylophone and x-ray are two common x-words. Don't worry too much about finding other words for this letter!

One step further

Play an alphabet game! You'll need two players or teams.

1. **Each team takes a turn sharing a word for each letter of the alphabet.** For example, one team starts with "A is for apple," and the other team starts with "A is for alligator." Then, "B is for book," and so on.

2. **Can't think of a word?** The winning team says, "Goodbye. See you next time."

3. **Two ways to win:** If the other team cannot think of a word, your team wins. If both teams find a word for every letter, you both win!

For more challenging gameplay, impose a time limit on how long a team has to come up with a word.

⑫ Go to Sleep Tonight

Overview

An adoring lullaby ends the album and allows young learners to apply the breadth of their newfound knowledge about times of day, repetition, prepositions, and so on.

Discover the song

A lullaby is usually a quiet, gentle song sung to help put a child to sleep. Tell learners to pay attention to musical elements, such as tempo (speed), dynamics (volume), and tone. Then ask them how the song makes them feel. Would they feel the same way after listening to a rock song?

Activity

Cut dreamy cloud shapes out of paper or poster board. Next, brainstorm how a lullaby makes you feel before bedtime. Write down each word on a cloud. Need some inspiration? Come up with opposites for the words below. Or look for ideas in some of the other songs!

Awake
Sad
Afraid
Mad
Scared

One step further

Create a lullaby mobile! Make at least three to five clouds. On the back of each cloud, draw a face to match the feeling written on the other side. Tape or tie strings of varying lengths onto each cloud. Then attach each string to a ring, hanger, or branch that you can hang above a crib or bed.

Singers Sunflowers (Julie Harris and Aaron Harris) Words and music Aaron Harris
Illustrations Maud Legrand Artistic Director Roland Stringer
Production, musical direction and arrangements Sunflowers Recorded by Sunflowers
Mixed by Bruno Pradels Mastering at Sonics Mastering Studio
Graphic design by Stéphan Lorti for Haus Design Activity guide by Michael Belcher
Copy Editor Katherine Sehl Musicians Aaron Harris Guitars and ukulele Julie Harris Harmonica
Nicolas Fleury Electric and upright bass Albertine Obert Violin and viola Lucas Baudon Cello

To our beautiful Alyssa Valentina and to all the boys and girls all around the world

A unique code for the digital download of all recordings and a printable file of the text and illustrations is included with this book-CD. All recordings are also available on several musical streaming platforms.

© ℗ 2022 The Secret Mountain (Folle Avoine Productions)
www.thesecretmountain.com
ISBN 978-2-925108-91-7

All rights reserved. No part of this publication may be reproduced or transmitted in any form or by any means, electronic or mechanical, including photocopying, recording or any information storage and retrieval system, without permission in writing from the publisher. Printed in China.